For my mom and dad

The illustrations in this book were made with pencils, pastels, crayons, and markers—and a little bit of Photoshop.

Cataloging-in-Publication Data has been applied for and may be obtained from the Library of Congress.

ISBN 978-1-4197-4182-1

Printed and bound in China

10 9 8 7 6 5 4 3 2 1

Abrams® is a registered trademark of Harry N. Abrams, Inc.

ABRAMS The Art of Books
195 Broadway, New York, NY 10007
abramsbooks.com

THIS JOY!

SHELLEY JOHANNES

ABRAMS BOOKS FOR YOUNG READERS

NEW YORK

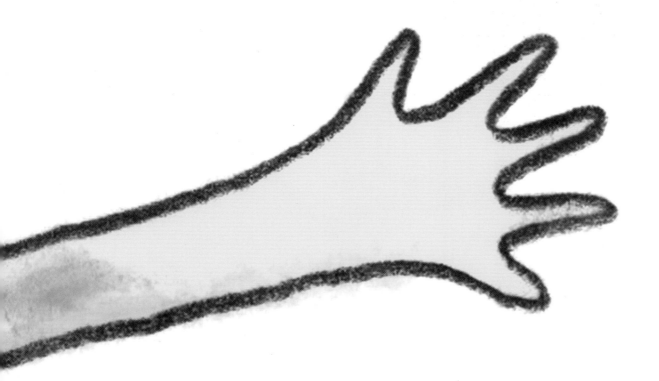

MY ARMS AREN'T
BIG ENOUGH

to HOLD THE WHOLE WORLD

with ALL its GREEN

AND ALL its BLUE . . .

BUT WHEN I FEEL
this HAPPY,
it's ALL
I WANt
to DO!

My
tiptoes
AREN'T
TALL
ENOUGH

to touch
THE TREETOPS

OR REACH
THE CLOUDS...

My legs aren't long enough to cover all the ground.

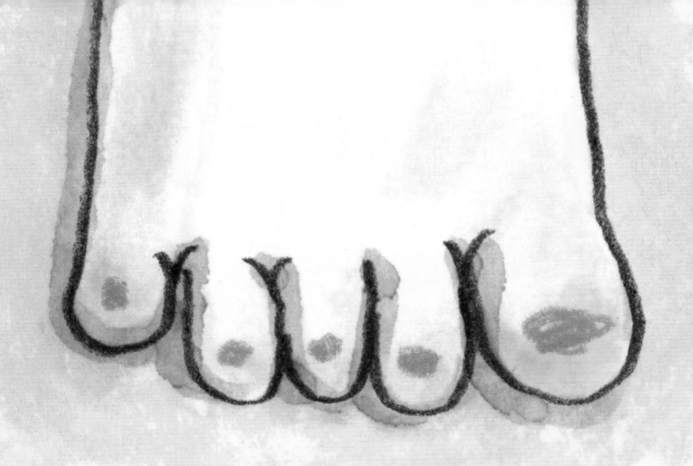

MY FEET CAN'T FEEL
EVERY GRAIN OF SAND

OR WADE INTO
EVERY INCH OF WILD.

I DON'T HAVE ENOUGH FINGERS
to COUNT ALL THE PEOPLE,

BUT I WISH WE COULD SHARE
A BILLION SMILES.

My voice isn't loud enough to express this joy!

EVEN WITH A MICROPHONE

OR A MEGAPHONE

AND MY FRIENDS
ON BACKUP XYLOPHONES.

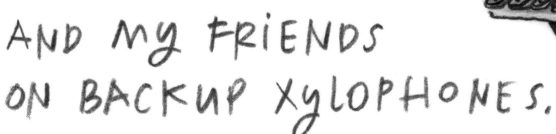

THE ALPHABET
DOESN'T HAVE
ENOUGH
LETTERS.

LETTERS DON'T HAVE ENOUGH SOUNDS.

EVEN WHEN I try
AND try AND try . . .

GiDDY

glorious

grateful

SPEECHLESS

MAYBE it's AN EXCLAMATION MARK!

OR THE KIND WHERE

EVERYONE SINGS ALONG.

is it BiRDS IN FLiGHt?

SQUiRRELS AT PLAy...

MAYBE it's A PIROUETTE

OR A HiLL WHERE I CAN ROLL.

today is a gift

MY ARMS CAN'T HOLD.

ALTHOUGH I'M SMALL,

my HEARt is tALL

AND MY ARMS
ARE EXACTLY
THE RIGHT SIZE...

FOR HOLDING you.